The
Snowman
Raymond Briggs

PUFFIN

Other books
by Raymond Briggs

FATHER CHRISTMAS
FATHER CHRISTMAS GOES ON HOLIDAY
JIM AND THE BEANSTALK
FUNGUS THE BOGEYMAN

Based on Raymond Briggs' original story

THE SNOWMAN AND THE SNOWDOG BOOK AND CD

PUFFIN BOOKS
Published by the Penguin Group: London, New York, Australia, Canada, India,
Ireland, New Zealand and South Africa
Penguin Books Ltd, Registered Offices: 80 Strand, London WC2R 0RL, England
puffinbooks.com
First published by Hamish Hamilton 1978
Published in Puffin Books 1980
Published in this edition 2013
001
Copyright © Raymond Briggs, 1978
Made and printed in China
ISBN: 978–0–723–27553–4

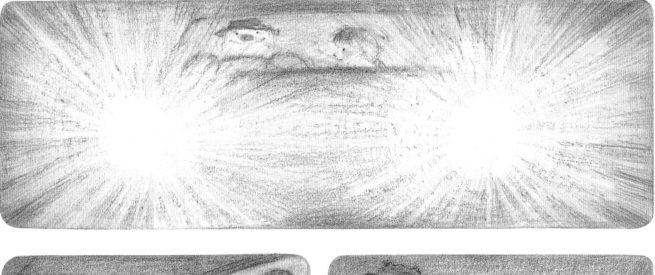

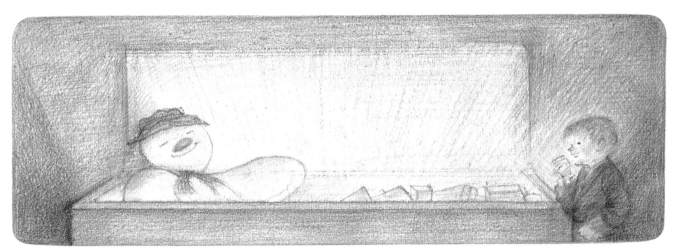

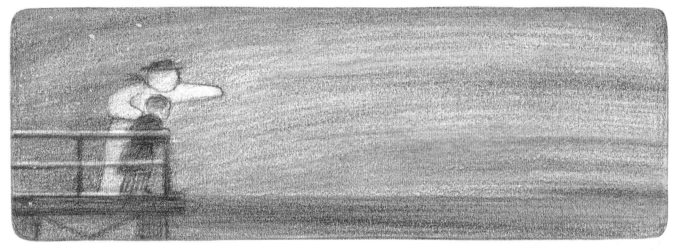

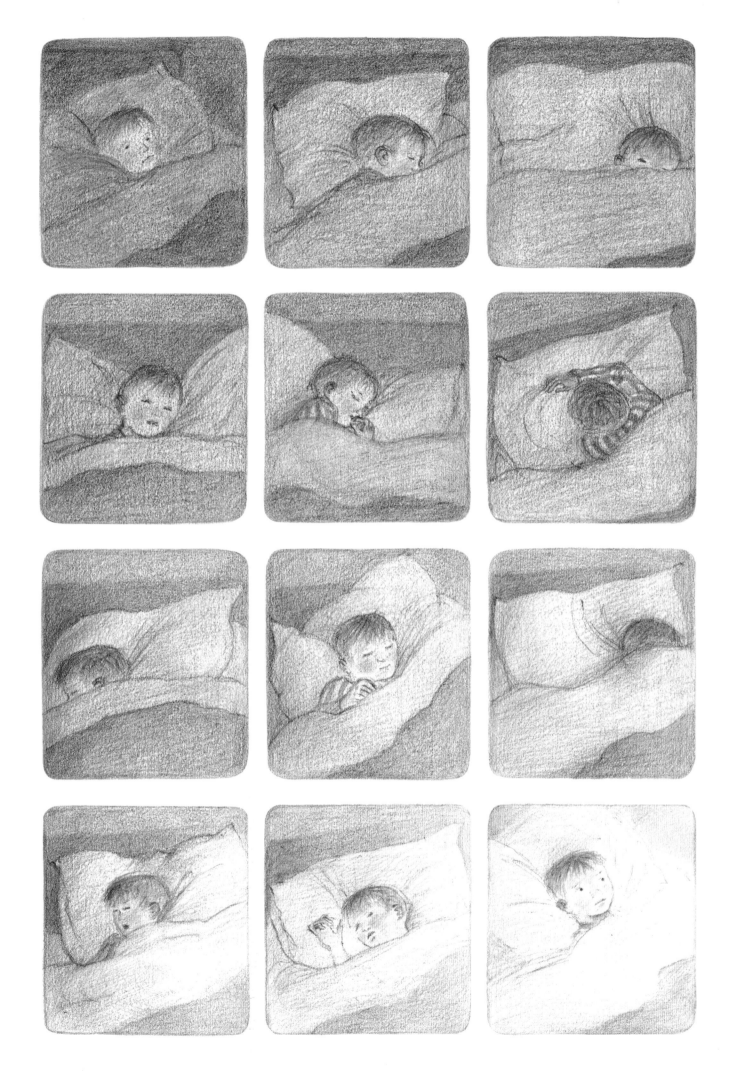